To my own little monsters,
Violet, Primrose, and Wisteria

A Feiwel and Friends Book
An imprint of Macmillan Publishing Group, LLC

TRUCKEROO SCHOOL. Copyright © 2017 by David Kirk. All rights reserved.
Printed in China by RR Donnelley Asia Printing Solutions Ltd., Dongguan City, Guangdong Province.
For information, address Feiwel and Friends, 175 Fifth Avenue, New York, N.Y. 10010.

Our books may be purchased in bulk for promotional, educational, or business use.
Please contact your local bookseller or the Macmillan Corporate and Premium Sales Department at
(800) 221-7945 ext. 5442 or by e-mail at MacmillanSpecialMarkets@macmillan.com.

Library of Congress Cataloging-in-Publication Data Available
ISBN: 978-1-250-01690-4

Book design by Patrick Collins

Feiwel and Friends logo designed by Filomena Tuosto

First Edition: 2017
The illustrations for this book were created using watercolor and gouache on Arches paper.

1 3 5 7 9 10 8 6 4 2

mackids.com

TRUCKEROO
SCHOOL

story and paintings by

DAVID KIRK

FEIWEL AND FRIENDS

NEW YORK

Everyone in Truckeroo
must drive a truck—the children, too.
The very day that kids are born,
they're handed tailpipes, wheels, a horn.
Before they make their diaper wet,
they build a friend, a truck—a pet!

Each monster child is made unique,
some short and stout, some long and sleek.

A truck should fit, as best can be,
its owner's personality.

So every truck is made from scratch
to be a friend—a perfect match.

Which pet is which? Please, try to choose.
Whose kid is that? Which truck is whose?

Here's little Budge, a healthy boy
with lots of dump truck to enjoy.
The seat alone holds seven tons,
enough to brace his bulky buns.
Its iron wheels can bear the stress
of pure humongous monstrousness.

Persmella—such a dainty lass,
admired for spewing stinky gas,
has built her truck to complement
the subtle flavors of her scent.
From down the road, you're sure to hear
foul vapors hissing front and rear.

And this is Smeve, a little clot
with temper raging fiery hot!
His truck is fitted with a spout
to blast his flaming tantrums out.
But when instead the truck gets mad,
its fits are fifty times as bad!

This monster mess, a boy called Tuk,
has cobbled up a patchwork truck
from ragged sheets of rumpled tin.
The wheels are loose, the pipes are thin.
Tuk's rags can't hide his underwear.
Both truck and trousers need repair.

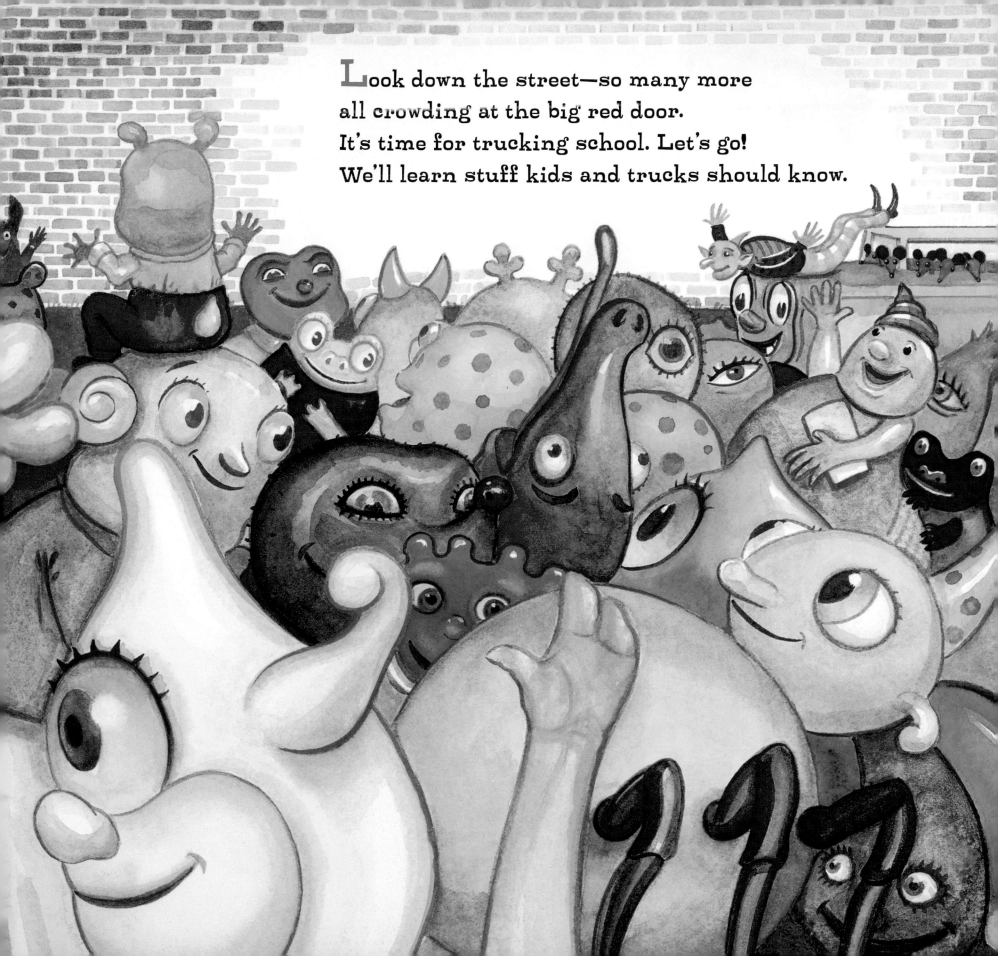

Look down the street—so many more
all crowding at the big red door.
It's time for trucking school. Let's go!
We'll learn stuff kids and trucks should know.

The day begins with exercise—
extending tires or flexing thighs.
They twirl or roll with kicks and tussles
to stretch their struts and tone their muscles.

And next, a class in making art.
A parking lot—the place to start.
They splash the pavement and the soil
with curls and swirls of engine oil,
then leave their tracks to sign their name.
The curb and grass supply the frame.

The teacher howls; the students squeal
and smack their desks with lumps of steel.
With horns all blasting out of tune,
this music class can't end too soon!

At recess, monsters take their fun,
with sport and games for everyone!
The children practice vaults and falls
and knock their noggins into walls.
The trucks bound over piles of rocks.
The kids pick pebbles from their socks.

Is it already time to eat?
Young monsters must have something sweet.
Their trucks however all require
meals that explode or catch on fire.
It's most delicious when it comes
from greasy tubs or metal drums.

How lucky that we're here today!
Careers with trucks are on display.
There's hauling oil and digging holes

or sticking signs on top of poles,
fine-tuning engines and repair
of all the gizmos under there.

NO CLIMBING!

OIL

A mom who flattens bumps and dents.
Another blows the bugs from vents.

A dad who puts out engine fires
and one who patches busted tires.

This one is little Budge's dad.
He's truckin' big and truckin' bad.
His axles higher than the trees,
the children's heads don't reach his knees.
He picks up kids in groups of ten—
I hope he puts them down again!

Now school is over. Time to go,
to practice all the stuff they know—
and very soon, as truck school grads
succeed just like their moms and dads.
They'll study very hard until
they're just like them . . .

but better still!

Come to Please come

You are car ~~corda~~ cordialy

You are car ~~corda~~ cordialy ~~time~~ rty.

Dear _____,

YOU ARE INVITED

by me (Georgie!) to

THE BEST PARTY EVER!

Love,

Georgie

To those who have ever felt lonely.
You are never as alone as you think.

Text copyright © 2016 by Ruth Chan

Published by Roaring Brook Press

Roaring Brook Press is a division of Holtzbrinck Publishing Holdings Limited Partnership

175 Fifth Avenue, New York, New York 10010

mackids.com

Library of Congress Cataloging-in-Publication Data

Names: Chan, Ruth, 1980- author, illustrator.

Title: Where's the party? / by Ruth Chan.

Other titles: Where is the party?

Description: First edition. | New York : Roaring Brook Press, 2016 |
    Summary: Georgie the cat loves to throw parties but this time,
    not one of his friends can come.

Identifiers: LCCN 2015029448 | ISBN 9781626722699 (hardcover)

Subjects: | CYAC: Parties—Fiction. | Friendship—Fiction. | Surprise—
    Fiction. | Animals—Fiction.

Classification: LCC PZ7.1.C477 Whe 2016 | DDC [E]—dc23

LC record available at http://lccn.loc.gov/2015029448

Our books may be purchased in bulk for promotional, educational,
or business use. Please contact your local bookseller or the Macmillan
Corporate and Premium Sales Department at (800) 221-7945 ext. 5442
or by e-mail at MacmillanSpecialMarkets@macmillan.com.

First edition, 2016

Book design by Kristie Radwilowicz

Printed in China by Toppan Leefung Printing Ltd.,

Dongguan City, Guangdong Province

10 9 8 7 6 5 4 3 2 1

"A PARTY WITHOUT CAKE IS JUST A MEETING."
—Julia Child

Where's the PARTY?

Ruth Chan

ROARING BROOK PRESS

NEW YORK

To Georgie, there was nothing better in the world than throwing a party for his friends.

Parties with balloons.

Parties with lights.

Parties with cake and frosting.

But, more than anything, parties where
everyone had a marvelous time.

One morning, Georgie woke up with the best of best ideas.
"Today would be a perfect day to throw a party!"

Georgie took a deep breath.
This had to be done just right.

Georgie knew his friends loved cake.
Georgie knew how much his belly loved cake, too.
And it wanted the biggest one.

Georgie checked his list.
He checked it again, just to be sure.
Now came his favorite part.

His best friend, Feta, was his go-to party pal.
But Feta couldn't come.

Georgie understood. Georgie liked pickles, and knew that a good pickle took time.

Lester lived down the street, and loved to dance
to Georgie's kazoo.
But Lester couldn't come either.

Georgie's whiskers drooped.
But no light meant bumping into things, and he
knew that was no fun.

Georgie was sure
Ferdinand would be
home. (He always was.)

Georgie sighed. He had tried his hardest, but
sometimes Ferdinand preferred to stay where he was.

A party was still a party, however small.

And there were still plenty of friends to ask.

But Sneakers was too busy . . .

. . . and it looked like Rocco
was already having a blast.

Georgie asked and asked until he had
no one left to ask.

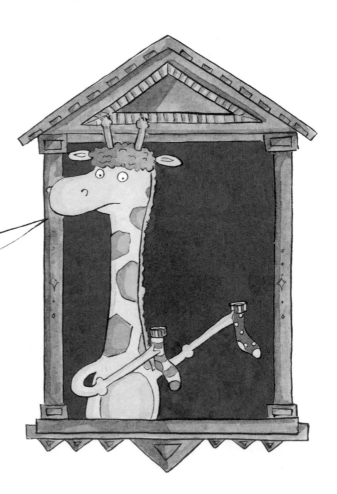

"Sounds fantastic, but the sidewalk is on the wrong side."

"I can't. My shorts are too bright."

Everyone had a reason for not being able to come.

Georgie stopped by Feta's
house again.
Surely he must be done
with his pickles by now.

But there were no pickles,
and no Feta.

And no more cake.

Maybe it wasn't the day for a party after all.
Maybe it was time to go home.

It was a long walk back.

But as Georgie came up his stoop, he saw . . .

. . . the most perfect party he'd ever seen!

It had balloons.

BOBBING FOR PICKLES

It had lights.

It even had more cake.

① PIN THE TAIL!
② THAT'S IT!

But best of all . . .

. . . it had all his friends.

Every single one of them.